JULIA JARMAN & ADRIAN REYNOLDS

BIG BLUE TRAIN

ORCHARD

Ben and Bella in the big blue train —
Huffa puffa, Chuffa Luffa!

Blow the whistle, Bella!

Pull the handle, Ben!

BIG BLUE TRAIN

**To Peter,
Theo, Maya, Faith, Lois,
Alfie, Hattie and Phoebe — J.J.**

For Tómas — A.R.

ORCHARD BOOKS
Carmelite House, 50 Victoria Embankment, London EC4Y, 0DZ
Orchard Books Australia
Level 17/207 Kent Street, Sydney, NSW 2000

First published in 2007 by Orchard Books
First published in paperback in 2008

ISBN 978 1 40835 603 6

Text © Julia Jarman 2007
Illustrations © Adrian Reynolds 2007

A CIP catalogue record for this book is available from the British Library.

5 7 9 10 8 6 4

Printed in China

Orchard Books is a division of Hachette Children's Books, an Hachette UK company.

www.hachettechildrens.co.uk

Chuffa Luffa puffs from the station, then . . .
Chugga chuff! Clickety clack!

Who's that waving
by the track?

"Hello, kids! Please help me —
I'm invited to a party at half-past three!"
"Jump on, Cat. We'll get you there
by half-past three with time to spare."

Cat jumps aboard in a single bound.

Chuffa Luffa's wheels go whizzing round.

Cat, Ben and Bella in the big blue train.
Huffa puffa, Chuffa Luffa!

Blow the whistle, Bella!

Pull the handle, Ben!

Chuffa Luffa steam train is off again.
Off to the North Pole — here we go!

But who's that stomping in the snow?

"Hi there, kids! Is there room for a bear?
I'm going to a party. Can you take me there?"
"Pile in, Polar. Sit by Cat,
and hold on tight to your party hat!"

Polar piles in. Sparks fly high!

Steam puffs up into the sky!

Chuffa Luffa steam train is off again!
We're chugging through the jungle,
one, two, three . . .

But who's
that leaping
from the tree?

"Hello, kids! Is there room for me?
I'm going to a party by the sea!"
"Oh yes, Leopard, there's room for you.
We're all going to the party too!"

Leopard leaps in — with two chimpanzees!

Move along now! You'll have to squeeze!

Leopard, Polar, Cat, Bella and Ben,
and the chimpanzees! We're off again!
Huffa puffa, Chuffa Luffa!
Huffa puffa, chugga chuffa.

Smoke billows!
Sparks fly high!

Steam puffs up
into the sky!

. . . clucky hen!
"Hello, kids! Will you take me
and my chicks to the birthday tea?"
"Yes, Clucky. Move along now!
But **NOT** you, Spotty Cow!"

But Spotty Cow climbs on . . .

and fills the truck!

Chuffa chugs to the desert ...

but then ... gets **STUCK!**

And Camel appears. "Sorry, Camel!
There isn't room for another mammal!"

"No, Camel! There isn't room!"
But Camel pushes Chuffa Luffa
who starts to . . .

Out of the tunnel — wheels spin fast!

Then Chuffa Luffa stops SUDDENLY!

"Jump out, we're here!" cries Chimpanzee.

But whose birthday is it?
Let's go and see!

It's Puppy Dog's!
"Hip-hip hooray!
Happy birthday to you, today!"

"Thank you, friends! Today I'm three!
Come and share my birthday tea.

There's birthday cake for everyone,
and birthday games, lots of fun!"

Then there's jumping over the foam,

till Clucky cries, "We must go home!"

Puppy Dog waves. "Thank you. Goodbye!"
As smoke puffs up into the sky.

Pile in the train! Hold on tight!
Hurry, Chuffa Luffa, through the night!"

Drop our friends off, on the way.
See you all another day!

Blow the whistle, Bella!

Pull the handle, Ben!

Now, Chuffa Luffa take us home again!

We're back at the station,
Chuffa Luffa's puffed out
after so much racing about.

And here comes Mum.
"Bedtime, you two."

"Goodnight, Chuffa Luffa, and thank you!"